DRAGON STORM 4

MIRA AND FLAMETELLER

Alastair Chisholm

illustrated by Eric Deschamps

A STEPPING STONE BOOK™

Random House 🏠 New York

CONTENTS

Text copyright © 2022 by Alastair Chisholm
Cover art and interior illustrations copyright © 2022 by Eric Deschamps

Visit us on the Web!
rhcbooks.com

Educators and librarians, for a variety of teaching tools, visit us at
RHTeachersLibrarians.com

Library of Congress Cataloging-in-Publication Data is available upon request.
ISBN 978-0-593-47963-6 (paperback) —
ISBN 978-0-593-47964-3 (library binding) — ISBN 978-0-593-47965-0 (ebook)

Printed in the United States of America
10 9 8 7 6 5 4 3 2 1
First American Edition

IN THE LAND OF DRACONIS, THERE ARE NO DRAGONS.

Once, there were. Once, humans
and dragons were friends and guarded
the land. They were wise, and strong, and
created the great city of Rivven together.

But then came the Dragon Storm, and the
dragons retreated from the world
of humans. To the men and women of
Draconis, they became legend and myth.

And so, these days, in the land of Draconis,
there are no dragons. . . .

Or so people thought.

1
MIRA

"Wake up!" shouted Mira. "Wake up, everyone. It's Wheel Day!"

She went to Erin's bed and shook her shoulder.

"Erin, it's Wheel Day!"

Erin, who had been fast asleep, growled. She peered at Mira with one bleary eye.

"It's *early*," she complained. "And there's no such thing as Wheel Day."

"There is!" shouted Mira happily. "And it's *today*! Come on!"

She ran to the third bed in their shared dorm hut. "Wake up, Cara!"

Cara was just a lump under her covers. "G'way," the lump muttered.

"But it's *Wheel Day*!" Mira laughed. "I'm going to help Hilda get breakfast ready, so we can set off early!"

"Mmmf," muttered Erin, and rolled over.

It *was* early, Mira admitted to herself as she left the dorm. The light was still dim, and there was no one around. In the outside world, the sun would just be rising . . . but not here. Because Mira, the dorm, and everything around her weren't in the outside world.

They were in the Dragonseer Guild Hall.

The Hall was a vast cavern, lit up by softly glowing globes that hung above like tiny suns. It held a training area, a racetrack, dormitories, dining huts, classrooms, offices, and more. Older buildings that were perfect for exploring could be seen off in the distance. It had everything Mira and her friends needed.

Mira closed her eyes, relaxed, and called up the special magic she had been taught on her first day as a dragonseer. She felt a whispering connection. . . .

And the dragon Flameteller appeared.

Flameteller was small, but still taller than Mira herself, with a stumpy body and a long neck. He was bronze and brown, like the colors of wood, with spots of silver. His legs were stiff and straight. He looked as if he was made of wood and brass, like a cleverly designed windup toy. Every time Mira saw him, her heart sang.

He stretched his wings with a click-click-click sound. "Good morning, Mira!" he chirped. "Is it Wheel Day today?"

Mira grinned. "Yes! But everyone else is sleeping in. I'm off to help Hilda with breakfast. Want to come?"

"Of course!"

Flameteller trotted beside her to one of the dining huts, where they found Hilda preparing breakfast. Hilda was strong-shouldered and tall. She always had her sleeves rolled up. She smiled at Mira and Flameteller as they entered the dining hut.

"You're up early, my loves!" she said.

"I couldn't sleep," said Mira. "It's Wheel Day! We're off to see the Rivven Wheel!"

Flameteller clicked his wings. "It's the biggest waterwheel in the *world*! It might be the biggest *machine* in the world! Mira's told me all about it."

"We thought we'd come and help with

breakfast," said Mira. "Nobody else is awake yet! Why would anyone sleep in on Wheel Day?"

"It's a mystery," said Hilda, smiling. "Well, some help would be lovely. Come on in, but wash your hands and face, Mira—you're covered in grease, as usual!"

Mira laughed and washed at the water pump, peering at her reflection in the hut window. Hilda was right. Mira's long black hair was tied into a ponytail with a greasy rag. Her soft brown skin was covered with streaks of black. Mira loved tinkering with machinery, and somehow always came away with grease marks on her skin and clothes.

She went into the hut and helped Hilda get

breakfast together. Even though he was small for a dragon, Flameteller was too large to fit in the hut, so Mira opened the window and he stuck his head through. The other children eventually wandered over. They yawned as Hilda and Mira served them breakfast. Then there was clearing away, and dishes, and finally—finally!—the others started getting ready. Mira was bursting with impatience!

At last they stood with their dragons in a semicircle around Lady Berin, Chancellor of the Dragonseer Guild.

Every dragon was different. That was one of the first things Mira had learned when she joined the Dragonseer Guild. She remembered the first time she saw the Guild Hall.

"The world of dragons is not like ours," Berin had told her. "It is a world of *ideas*. When a dragon first steps into our world, they find their form, and that depends on the dragonseer who summons them. They are your dragon, and you are their human."

And just as every dragon was unique, so was their *power*—the special magic that they, and only they, could do. Some had discovered their powers already. The dragon that Tom summoned was Ironskin, a large, powerful creature the color of flames and hammered iron. She could create a shield to protect others.

Ellis's stumpy green dragon, Pathseeker, was clever and practical. She could see through illusions. Cara's dragon, Silverthief, could turn invisible for a while. Others were still figuring out their powers—like Flameteller. Mira knew that Kai and his white-and-red dragon, Boneshadow, and Connor and Lightspirit were still waiting to find out their powers. Poor Erin was still getting the hang of summoning and needed help to bring her enormous dragon, Rockhammer, into the human world.

"Is everyone ready for our trip?" asked Berin. Mira and Flameteller nodded vigorously, and the others laughed.

Berin smiled. "Well, Mira, why don't you lead the way?"

Mira grinned and set off toward the doors

at the far end of the Hall. As she reached them, Flameteller said, "Time for me to go."

Mira nodded and gently bumped heads with her dragon. Then Flameteller faded from sight. Around her, the other children smiled and waved to their own dragons, too, as each one disappeared.

"Flame?" whispered Mira.

Hello! came Flameteller's voice in her head, and Mira smiled.

They left the Hall and walked along the twisting passageways that led out to the city. These were the Clockwork Corridors, and Mira loved them. They were part of the protections of the Guild. The Clockwork

Corridors were like a maze that moved under their feet. The maze was actually a clever machine to fool anyone trying to enter the Dragonseer Guild. Floor tiles slotted into place around them, doors and passages opened ahead, and Mira felt the thrum of machinery under her feet. At last they reached the exit, hidden in a small cottage.

They left the cottage and stepped out into the city of Rivven.

2
THE RIVVEN WHEEL

Rivven was the largest city in Draconis, and the oldest. Its streets and houses pushed and piled on top of each other. Narrow lanes squeezed between houses, markets, tanners, merchant halls, and smithies. Above it all sat the gleaming white walls of the Royal Palace atop the mighty Palace Rock.

Berin marched her students through the bustling streets. Occasionally, rich merchants or city leaders nodded to Lady Berin, and she nodded back. Out on the streets Lady Berin was a city magistrate. Almost no one knew her secret role as head of the Dragonseer Guild. Officially, the children were apprentice clerks, and they wore their brown apprentice cloaks and followed as well as they could.

They left through the South Gate, and Berin led them along the road toward the southern hills. She was tall and walked in brisk, long strides, and the children had to trot to keep up.

"This way!" she called. "Oh, isn't it nice to breathe some fresh air?"

At the back of the group, Connor groaned.

"How much *farther*? It's been miles!" Connor wasn't much of an outdoor person. His idea of happiness was to be curled up with a book, ignoring everything else.

Erin laughed. "It's been one mile, if that, slow-bones!" Erin was tall and athletic and went running *for fun*. She towered over Mira and positively glowed with health. She and Connor almost never agreed on anything. Connor muttered something under his breath and continued walking.

"Come on!" Mira called, skipping ahead. "It's just over this hill! Race you!"

Erin grinned and chased after her. Mira reached the top and gazed down into a small valley. From the south came the deep and fast-moving River Seek, driving between the hills toward Rivven. But halfway along, an ancient stone channel forced the river down to a single point, furious and spitting, until it thundered over a huge, ancient waterwheel.

The Rivven Wheel.

The wheel was vast. Its spokes were huge beams of oak, pitted with centuries of use. Its blades were enormous, and the huge iron pins that held it in place were wide and long. As it turned, it made a *SH-SH-SH* sound, on and on, while the river roared and the axle creaked.

"Oh . . . ," gasped Mira. "It's *beautiful*."

Erin glanced at her. "It's just a big wheel."

It IS beautiful! came Flameteller's excited voice in Mira's mind, and she smiled. Berin started down the hill, and Mira scurried after her.

Next to the wheel were a collection of large

work buildings, wet from the river and thick with moss, but made of strong, neat bricks. An old man waited outside. He was dressed in brown boots, a brown coat, and a shapeless brown hat. He had wide shoulders and a square jaw. He was smiling.

"Afternoon, Your Ladyship," he said, removing his hat and bowing.

"Good afternoon, Joshua," said Berin. "Thank you for letting us visit. Students, this is Joshua, and he is our guide. Listen to what he says. Do not touch anything or go anywhere without checking with him. A waterwheel can be very dangerous!"

"Come on in, young'uns," he said, and led

the group of dragonseers into a brick building next to the waterwheel.

The wheel turned under the force of the rushing water, its pulleys and cogwheels transferring power to other places. There was a mill, grinding wheat into fine flour between two huge stones. There was a factory, crushing rocks from a nearby lead mine. There was even a mechanical hammer, pounding sheets of iron. Everywhere around them rang with the sound of industry and the roar of the wheel.

Joshua showed the children around. Tom, whose father was a blacksmith, was interested in the hammer; Kai, who loved animals and nature, looked a bit bored. But Mira stared at everything with her mouth hanging open in wonder. She felt the thrum of the works beneath her feet and heard the whir of pulleys and the clank of gears, and almost laughed with delight.

"Wonderful!" she gasped.

Erin rolled her eyes. "You're so weird." But she was grinning, and Mira grinned back.

Finally Joshua led them into a smaller room at the back, with thick walls that calmed the sound of machinery to a quiet drone. He closed the door behind them and nodded to Berin. She stepped forward.

"Students," she said quietly. She looked very serious. "The Dragonseer Guild must stay secret, but we do have friends, here and there." She bowed to Joshua, and he smiled. "And there's something we'd like to show you today."

Joshua led them over to the hearth. Taking a rag, he rubbed away the brick dust to reveal a mark carved into the stone: three short vertical lines.

"Who can tell me what this means?" asked Berin.

Connor said, "It's *dragon,* miss. It means it's dragon-made."

Berin smiled. "That's right."

Dragons? asked Flameteller's voice. *We made this?*

Berin faced the group. "You are *dragonseers.* Each of you has the power to allow a dragon into this world. It is a wonderful thing, but these days, a dangerous thing too. We all know what humans think of dragons. We know that many are scared. There are wild stories and false histories.

"But once, dragons and humans worked together. This waterwheel is an ancient wonder—over a thousand years old, one of the first devices built by humans and dragons together. And this is their mark."

The children gazed at the carved lines until Berin nodded again to Joshua, and he took a handful of dust and rubbed it over the brickwork.

"Now," she said, "are there any questions?"

Mira's hand shot
up.

"Yes, what is the
maximum capacity at
the headrace?"

Berin blinked. "Er . . .
the what?"

"The point where
the water goes onto
the wheel," said Mira.
"What's the maximum
capacity? How do you cope with overflow?"

"Well—"

"Ooh, how much force does it generate?
Why does it use a backshot system? Is it for

improved efficiency? How often do you have to replace the blades? Is there a reason they're shaped like that? What does—"

Berin raised a hand. "Well, I really meant about the *history* of the building. But if Joshua doesn't mind, I'm sure he can answer your questions, Mira. And since that may take a while"—the others laughed—"the rest of us will eat lunch on the hillside in the meantime."

They left, leaving just Joshua and Mira.

"Now, miss," said Joshua, smiling. "What would you like to know?"

Mira's eyes gleamed.

"*Everything.*"

Mira chatted nonstop as they walked back to the city. "And the wheel runs toward the top of the headrace to reduce turbulence, see, and the blades are at that angle because it lets them catch the water and release it quickly. Did you know this waterwheel used to power a rail cart? It pulled it all the way up from Riven! And—"

"Argh!" shouted Erin. "The only thing more boring than that wheel is you going on about it!"

Mira stopped. "What? But it was *brilliant*! You know, the Guild Hall must use a lot of power. All the moving walkways and the lights. How does that work? Lady Berin, does the Guild have a waterwheel?"

Ahead of them, Berin shook her head. "No, Mira. We have something else. Perhaps one day you can see."

"Cool!"

It was late afternoon when they reached the city gate again.

"Well, children," said Berin. "I hope you enjoyed that. Remember—no matter what you hear, there was a world once where dragons and humans were friends. It's our job to make that world again."

But just inside the gate, she stopped, staring up at a huge banner strung between two buildings. Mira followed her gaze. Then her mouth dropped open in dismay.

"Oh, no," she murmured.

3
DRAGON
SCOURGE

The banner had a picture of a horrible, fierce dragon, breathing fire. Next to the dragon was a man wearing a crown and armor, holding a long spear. He was stabbing the dragon, and the dragon was writhing in agony.

DEATH TO DRAGGUNS, read the sign.

Is that supposed to be us? asked Flameteller's voice. Mira nodded.

There was a buzz of activity around them.

Posters had been pinned up all around, and Mira heard shouting up ahead. Berin's face was grim.

"Stay close to me, students," she said. "And remember: if anyone asks, you are apprentice clerks."

They walked toward the King's Plaza, an open square that was sometimes a marketplace, sometimes a festival area. Today there was a stage with red-and-gold drapes. A crowd was gathering. To the side sat a black carriage with four beautiful black horses. The carriage had no crest or other markings, and its curtains were closed.

A herald stepped onto the stage.

"My good people of Rivven!" he called in a barrel-chested roar.

The crowd stopped chattering and turned. The herald held up a scroll. "I bring a proclamation from His Majesty, King Godfic! He instructs me on this day to tell you—"

"I'll handle this," called a voice, and the herald stopped in surprise. Mira realized the carriage door had opened and a hooded figure now stood next to it. The figure leaped lightly onto the stage, patted the startled man on the back, and lifted his hood.

It was Prince Harald, the king's son! He handed his hooded cloak to his personal attendant. The crowd gasped, and many of them knelt, but he waved them back to their feet.

"No, no," he said. "Thank you, but I am not your king. Please, stand."

Prince Harald was rather handsome, Mira thought. He had shoulder-length blond hair and a friendly face. He wore a red outfit decorated with silver thread patterns. He smiled as the people stood again.

"As you know," he said, "my father counts the safety of Rivven and the land of Draconis above all things. He protects us from evil. But there are rumors of a danger from our past, come to haunt us again."

His voice was serious, and as he looked around, the people stayed hushed.

"I am talking about dragons," he said.

Mira gasped. Beside her, Berin pursed her lips but showed no other expression.

"We had not wanted to believe it," said the prince. "But recently an item under royal protection was stolen from the king's own chambers. It was a tool of old magic. Old *dragon magic*. And it can only be used by those who are in league with dragons."

There was a burst of excited chatter, but Prince Harald spoke over it.

"There are those who have chosen to side with dragons, against their own kind!" he roared. "They pretend to be your friends, but secretly they bring back these terrible creatures! They are here in Rivven—perhaps in this very square!"

Everyone in the crowd looked around, peering into each other's faces, searching for guilt. Berin's face stayed calm, and she gazed at the prince as if mildly interested in a curious idea. Mira and the others tried to copy her. The city, normally so friendly and bustling, suddenly felt very hostile.

"My father, King Godfic, Dragon Scourge,

is sworn to protect Draconis," continued Prince Harald. "And he has ordered me to root out these traitors! We will search every building in this city, and we will not stop until we have found them *and* their terrible creatures . . . and *destroyed* them! Who's with me?"

The crowd *roared* with a mix of anger and delight. They cheered and thumped each other on the backs.

Berin sighed. "This is no place for children," she said primly. "Come along."

She led them away from the square.

"That's all *lies*!" snapped Erin. "Why would he say that?"

"Quiet now," murmured Berin. "We'll discuss it later."

I don't like this, said Flameteller's voice in Mira's mind. He sounded worried. *The humans are scared of us. Scared humans do strange things.*

They passed the black carriage, and Mira saw another man standing there, dressed in the traditional black cloak of a clerk. It was Malik. He lived in the palace as the king's clerk. He was also, secretly, a member of the Dragonseer Guild. He brought them warnings. Now his face was pale and shocked. He tried to smile when he saw them.

"Clerk Malik," said Berin formally.

"Lady Berin," he said, bowing. "You are back from your trip, I see. Did my young apprentices enjoy their history lesson?"

"I think we are learning all sorts of things today," said Berin.

Malik nodded. "I will be in touch, my lady, to discuss their schedules. It might be a good time to take a short vacation. . . ."

Berin smiled. "Perhaps. Good day, Malik."

He bowed again, and she led the children back toward the cottage and the secret entrance to the Guild Hall.

"They must be talking about the Dragon's Eye," Tom said to Ellis as they walked. The Dragon's Eye was a magical jewel that

Ellis had seen during the Maze Festival last month.

Ellis nodded. "Yes. But it was the princess who took it, not us!"

"Maybe someone should tell the king," suggested Connor.

"No," said Berin. "We cannot place the princess in that situation. Besides . . ." She sighed. "This isn't about the Eye. King Godfic is determined to wipe out dragons, and the Eye is just his latest excuse. He wants to whip the crowd up into fear and use that."

"And Prince Harald?" asked Mira.

Berin shrugged. "As prince, he must follow his father's orders. Here we are."

She led the children into the narrow

side alley and toward the tiny, broken-down
cottage that hid the Guild Hall entrance.
Carefully checking around, they entered the
cottage and approached a plain cupboard
door. Mira felt a faint whir beneath her feet,
then heard a click, and the passageway
opened. The door clicked shut
behind them, and the hallway
moved.

This time Mira was too
worried to think about
the machinery, and
even the passageways
seemed to feel it.
They stuttered
and bumped.

Berin frowned as she waited for the last path to lurch into position.

They finally reached the large doorway at the end of the passages. Berin raised her staff. Blue light shimmered, and the door opened. They stepped through the doorway, returning to the safety of the Hall.

Mira felt a tremble in the air beside her, and the brown-bronze shape of Flameteller appeared. He nuzzled his head against her shoulder, his skin smooth like polished wood.

"It's all right," he said softly. "And the wheel was fun, wasn't it?"

"Mmm," said Mira. She forced a smile, but she was worried.

4
ANOTHER
WAY

Being back in the Guild Hall and seeing Flameteller made Mira feel better. Soon they were chatting away.

"Don't worry," she said. "Prince Harald's mob won't get anywhere near you. We'll build a machine to stop them, or something. Something enormous!" Flameteller laughed.

There was more laughing over dinner in the children's shared dining hut. Hilda had made spicy stew and dumplings. The young dragonseers joked with one another as they ate. They stopped worrying about everything going on outside.

Later, Berin summoned them to the training ground. She looked serious but not worried. Beside her were Daisy, who taught self-defense, and Creedy, the grim and scowling Vice Chancellor.

When everyone was there, Berin smiled.

"Students," she said. "You may be worried about the scene we saw outside. There is fear, and sometimes that can spread."

Mira remembered Flameteller's words. *Scared humans do strange things.*

"These things will pass," said Berin. "I believe that people, on the whole, are good. Eventually we *will* persuade them. But for now, we'll lie low. We'll stay here, safe in the Guild Hall. Continue your training, and step outside again when things have calmed down."

"But what if they find the entrance?" asked Ellis. "Prince Harald said he was going to search every building."

Berin smiled. "The Clockwork Corridors will protect us. Whenever the prince or his knights come close, we can simply move the passages away."

"What if he finds us anyway?" asked Erin.

"Will there be a fight?" She sounded a little too excited by that idea. By now, someone had helped her summon her gigantic dragon, Rockhammer, and he bristled his enormous spiky back.

"Let me at 'em," he growled.

Berin raised a hand. "There won't be a fight. This Hall"—she waved up at it—"is just a place. We can always find another." She paused before going on. "You all know about the Dragon Storm," she said. "Humans fought against humans, dragons against dragons. And afterward the dragons were so appalled they left us for hundreds of years. I won't let that happen again." She shook her head. "No. If Prince Harald were to discover us, the dragons would return to their own world, and we would remain in ours. The Hall and all of its history may be lost . . . but we will survive."

"Is there another way out?" Connor asked.

Berin smiled. "There is another way. There is a part of these caves you have not seen yet, and I will show you."

The children murmured. Ellis, who loved exploring and mapmaking, muttered excitedly to his dragon, Pathseeker. Only Erin seemed disappointed there wouldn't be a battle.

"Follow me!" called Berin, and she marched past the group and toward a cluster of storerooms. Inside, the rooms were piled with sacks and barrels, and shelves reached high with tools and other equipment—

everything needed to keep the Dragonseer Guild running. Berin walked to a half-hidden door at the back. It opened into another room, with a large rectangular hole in the floor and a ladder leading down. Mira heard water lapping against stone and felt a cool breeze against her face. As she reached the bottom of the ladder, she realized they were on a small dock beside an underground canal.

Ellis gasped in surprise. "I never knew *this* was here!"

Mira peered around. There were coils of rope and pulleys, and she felt the rumble of machinery. The sides of the canal were built of solid stone slabs. On the far side of the canal, the slabs stretched up to form a huge wall. Mira thought she heard rushing water.

"I think that's the River Seek on the other side of that wall," muttered Ellis. He was furiously scribbling notes. "This canal must come off it and then rejoin."

A boat came toward them out of the dark, pulled by a rope on a turning wheel. Hilda stood at the prow. Behind her sat Drun, a short man with a bushy gray beard and a leather jerkin. He gave them a cheery wave.

"Hilda," called Berin. "I've brought you and Drun some assistants."

Hilda grinned. "Good timing! We have some supplies to unload!"

The boat pulled in, and Hilda stepped out and tied it to a post.

"This is how we bring in everything we

48

need to keep the Guild running," said Berin. "Hilda manages this area, and we all take turns helping." She smiled. "And for a while you'll help too."

"This is the real heart of the Guild!" said Drun. He chuckled. "Or at least the belly, eh?"

"So you see," said Berin. "We have all we need. And even if Prince Harald somehow finds the entrance above, we have a way out. We'll be safe. Now! We have supplies to store, and you can all help."

Hilda and Drun unloaded small barrels, sacks, legs of salted ham, bags of spices, and casks of fresh water. The children and dragons carried them to a pallet. Mysterious machinery high above them heaved the pallets up to the supply room. Mira and Flameteller watched it curiously.

"Where *does* all the power come from?" Mira asked.

Berin's eyes twinkled. "Would you like to find out?" she asked.

"Yes!"

"Good! Because I have a special job for you, Mira. Come with me."

She led Mira away from the dock, to an area blocked by a large wall with a small, heavy door.

"You wanted to know how we power the Guild?" said Berin. "It's through here." She opened the door and entered. Mira and Flameteller followed.

5
GRIMBAL

Their mouths had fallen open in wonder. Berin, Mira, and Flameteller were in a machinery room, like the heart of the Rivven Wheel—but many times larger and busier! Pulleys squealed, wheels spun, gears crashed and meshed, pistons clattered. Above them, conveyor belts trundled and clanged. The whole room seemed to tremble with energy.

"Oh, *wow!*" Mira cried.

"This is *amazing*!" said Flameteller. His eyes glittered as he watched. Mira gazed up at the machinery around her, and for a moment it felt as if she was back in her father's workshop.

Mira's father was a clockmaker and always had dozens of clocks ticking, whirring, and chiming around him. For as long as she could remember, Mira had loved to sit on his lap as he showed her his latest mechanical creations. Mira would look up at the clocks and feel that she could never be happier.

But one day, when she was in the workshop by herself, daydreaming and listening to the machinery, she'd heard something new— a mysterious half-ticking, half-purring, half-mechanical, half-alive sound. And in among the mess of clockfaces and workings, she'd seen two small lights, almost like eyes, seeming to gaze back at her.

That had been six months ago, before Malik, the king's clerk, had unexpectedly come to visit and offered to make Mira an apprentice clerk. She hadn't been sure she wanted to leave, until he'd secretly explained the truth—that Mira was a *dragonseer*, someone who could reach into the world of dragons and connect to them. She'd met Drun, who had helped her learn how to summon. Then she'd seen Flameteller, rising out of the fire in Drun's hut, with his gorgeous brown-and-bronze coloring and his strange way of moving, almost like machinery. A creature of magic, shaped by his link to Mira and her love of all mechanical things. And every day since had felt more extraordinary than the last.

She wished she could show her father Flameteller and tell him about all the things she'd seen. Perhaps one day she could bring him to this incredible room! But for now, she looked at Flameteller's delighted face instead and laughed. Flameteller laughed with her.

"Amazing!" he said again.

"This way!" said Berin.

At the end of the room was another door. A hand-painted sign in yellow and black read:

ENGINE ROOM
DO NOT ENTER

Berin led them through the door and into the engine room.

Inside, there was a workbench, some shelves, a chair, and a few large metal levers in the corner. But the first thing Mira noticed was an enormous wheel, made of brass and iron, mounted flat against the far wall. The wheel turned. There was a design forged on the front of the wheel, the same three short lines they'd seen on the Rivven Wheel. *This* wheel was dragon-made too.

Mira gazed at it. The wheel turned slowly, but somehow with mighty power. The metal seemed to *thrum* with energy, like a huge coiled spring or a wild animal. Cautiously, she reached toward it—

"Don't touch that!"

Mira snatched her hand back and whirled. Behind them was a man with messy gray hair. He wore a leather jerkin over a tan shirt along with brown boots. His face was pulled down into a scowl. He looked as if he scowled a lot. His forehead was one big, angry wrinkle.

"That's a powerful and delicate device. Leave it alone!"

"Sorry!" squeaked Mira. "I was just—"

"You could have been hurt!" the man snapped. "Or even worse—you could have *damaged* it! What are you doing here?"

"I brought them," said Berin gently. "Hello, Grimbal."

The man seemed to notice Berin for the first time, and stopped.

"Yer Ladyship," he said in a grudging voice. "What can I do for you?"

"I'd like to introduce you," said Berin. "Mira, Flameteller, this is Grimbal. You asked how the Guild Hall works and where the power comes from. The answer is Grimbal. He is the genius who keeps everything going."

Grimbal's face softened slightly, although he still looked suspicious.

"And these," said Berin, "are Mira and Flameteller, both promising engineers themselves."

"Hello!" said Mira.

"Hmmph," muttered Grimbal.

"I thought they could assist you for a while," said Berin.

Grimbal blinked. "I don't need an assistant," he said, looking outraged. "I got everything going just right!"

"Of course," said Berin smoothly. "Only . . . there are some problems with the passageways, I think? Sticking sometimes?"

"Oh," said Grimbal, waving a hand. "I just got to get into the mechanism there—"

"And the lights have been flickering recently," said Berin.

"Well, you know, the lights is old. Sometimes they—"

"And I have wondered if the fans have been sometimes spinning loose?"

"Well, I can't do everything!" he protested. "I got a million jobs you don't even *know* about. I got to keep this place going, I got to repair it, I got—"

Berin raised her hands to stop him. "Absolutely, Grimbal. I understand you're very overworked. And so I've brought you two assistants."

"But—" Grimbal stopped. He opened his mouth once or twice, then closed it into a new scowl. "Yes, Yer Ladyship."

"Good!" Berin gave her widest smile. "Mira, Flameteller: Grimbal here is the best engineer I've ever met. He will teach you how all of this works, but you must do what he says, and *only* what he says. Understand?"

Mira and Flameteller glanced at each other. Grimbal still looked very grumpy. But there was a workshop . . . and this engine room . . . and the brass wheel . . . !

"Yes," said Flameteller.

"Absolutely," said Mira.

"Good!" said Berin. "Well, then, I'll leave you to it. Good luck!"

She left, leaving Mira, Flameteller, and Grimbal looking awkwardly at each other. Eventually Grimbal sighed.

"Well, you'll need some proper overalls," he said at last. "Come on."

6
THE DRAGON'S HEART

Grimbal found some old overalls in a back closet. Many of them were far too large for Mira, but he found a smaller pair and handed them to her.

"Right," he said. "Let's get to work."

Mira was very excited. "So is *everything* powered from here?"

"Yep."

"Even the Clockwork Corridors? The lights? Everything?"

"Yep."

"So where does the power come from?" asked Flameteller. "Is it from that big wheel? What *is* that?"

Grimbal sighed. "S'pose I'd better show you. But no touching, right?"

He opened a brass panel next to the wheel. Inside was a dial with three raised lines: the dragon mark. Grimbal reached into his deep pockets and pulled out a tool that looked like a wrench, with a head that fitted over the lines. He heaved the wrench, and the dial turned. A line formed down the disk in the center of the wheel. And suddenly Mira could see that the disk consisted of two parts, so neatly fitted together that they seemed like one. When the two parts separated, Mira saw something that *glowed*.

It shone like a diamond in sunlight, but as if the light was coming from inside it. It was a crystal, with flat sides and sharp lines. It throbbed like a living thing. It pulsed bright and soft, bright and soft.

"Oh . . . ," gasped Mira.

Grimbal nodded. "There are pieces of

magic in this world," he said. "No one's sure where from, but folk say they're fragments of the Dragon Realms. There are Dragon's Eyes, that let you see hidden things—"

"Oh, we know about them!" said Mira in a rush. "Ellis and Pathseeker found a girl who—"

Grimbal looked cross. Mira realized she'd interrupted his speech. "Sorry."

He cleared his throat. "*As I was saying*, there are Dragon's Eyes, that let you see hidden things. And there's Dragon's Blood, that they say can give you strength, and Dragon's Breath, rarest of all. . . . Well, this is the Dragon's Heart. Everything here—the Clockwork Corridors, the fans that give us fresh air, the barge pulley, even the lights—they're all powered by this."

"Like a waterwheel," murmured Flameteller. "The Heart turns the wheel, and the wheel turns everything."

Grimbal gave a thin smile. "There ain't a waterwheel in the world as powerful as the Dragon's Heart," he said proudly.

Mira gazed at it. "And you *built* this?"

"What? Oh, goodness, no. Look at the mark!" He pointed to the pattern of three lines. "No, this was dragon-made. A thousand years ago, maybe longer. No. I keep her going, though. Look after her."

The light wasn't completely even. One

patch seemed darker, about the size of Mira's hand.

"What's that dark patch?" she asked.

Grimbal sniffed. "Nothing." He closed the sliding panels with a *clang*.

Mira frowned. "It looked like there was something—"

"It's *nothing*," he snapped. "This old thing's been runnin' for over a thousand years. After the Dragon Storm, she was all by *herself*, without anyone to look after her, until we found her again. You try working a thousand years; you'll have a bit of wear and tear yourself!"

"Sorry," said Mira hurriedly. "I didn't mean—"

67

"Kids these days," muttered Grimbal. "They come in wet behind the ears, and suddenly they're telling you how to do your job!"

Mira and Flameteller glanced at each other's ears, but they seemed dry.

"Sorry?" tried Mira.

"Hmmph," he muttered again. "Right. Well, let's get to work."

Mira brightened. "What should we do first? The passageways? They were sticking when we came in. Or maybe the lights? Or should we—"

"That workbench," said Grimbal firmly. Mira looked at the old wooden workbench, piled high with old machine parts, ropes, cans, and tools.

"You can start by tidying it up."

The rest of the day was incredible!

And frustrating.

And amazing!

And boring.

The engine room powered the whole Guild Hall: every single light and mechanical device within it. The Dragon's Heart's slow but incredibly powerful turns drove huge gear wheels, which turned smaller ones, which pulled conveyor belts and spun crankshafts and moved walkways and carried lifts and heaved ropes and, oh, it was the most *amazing* thing Mira and Flameteller had ever seen!

But they hardly got a chance to examine it because they were tidying so much.

When they'd finished, Grimbal showed them the Clockwork Corridors control room, where mighty springs and levers shifted the maze that protected the Guild Hall from intruders!

He handed Mira a broom and told her to sweep up.

Then he repaired one of the globes that somehow took the mechanical energy from the Dragon's Heart and turned it into light!

Flameteller held the tools.

"There's all this *stuff*!" Mira complained later during dinner. "And it needs repairing. We could help, but all we're doing is *sweeping*!"

Erin shrugged. She crammed an entire bread roll into her mouth.

"You've just started, though," she said in a muffled voice.

"But Grimbal won't let us help! He doesn't even *like* us! Oh, Erin, you should have seen it!"

"We were too busy heaving barrels all afternoon," said Erin.

"Oh." Mira realized she hadn't asked about everyone else's day. "Sorry, that was probably much more boring."

Erin chuckled. "Actually, I quite enjoyed it. I can lift a barrel all by myself. Did you know that?" She raised an arm and flexed her muscles. "Connor tried, but he couldn't manage." At the end of the table, Connor bristled.

"Well, *some* of us are smart enough to roll them, aren't we?" he snapped. "Instead of showing off!"

"You *tried* to lift it. I saw you!" laughed Erin. The two dragonseers started bickering.

Mira left them to it. Erin and Connor always found a reason to argue, and sometimes it was fun, but she was too tired to join in this evening. She wandered back to their dorm hut and climbed onto the roof, where the children sometimes liked to sit. Then she cleared her mind and summoned Flameteller. There was a soft *thump* as the dragon appeared and settled down next to her.

"Oh, Flame," she murmured. "Wasn't it exciting!"

"Did you see the big cogwheels turn!" exclaimed the dragon.

Mira leaned against Flameteller's warm side and gazed up at the lights as they talked about the engine room, and the wheel, and Grimbal. It was nearing nightfall now, and the globes above her had dimmed, like stars. But, as she watched, one seemed to stutter. It went dark, then came back. Mira frowned.

"Did you think there was something odd about the Dragon's Heart?" she asked.

Flameteller nodded. "I could hear it, I think," he said. "It was like a note out of tune."

"Grimbal seemed angry I even asked."

"Perhaps once we've shown him what good engineers we are, he'll trust us more. It was only the first day."

"Yeah." Mira suddenly gave a wide yawn. "G'night, Flame."

"Good night, Mira."

Mira dragged herself to her feet, and Flameteller faded away. Mira could feel him in the back of her mind, half in the human world and half out. She smiled, clambered down, and headed back to her dorm.

How's Eliza doing? asked Flameteller's voice in her head.

Mira smiled and set her lantern on the windowsill beside her bed. There was a tiny spider, sitting at the edge of a web that spread several inches wide. Mira and Flameteller had watched her build it. Mira loved the way the little spider's web grew, and how perfectly she laid each strand and balanced each tension point. Eliza was a miniature marvel of engineering.

"Night night, Eliza," murmured Mira. She blew out the lamp and settled down. "Night night, Flame."

Night night, Mira, murmured Flameteller's voice, and Mira drifted to sleep.

7

FIXING

Berin, Creedy, and the other adults prepared for a possible siege by Prince Harald, and the young dragonseers and their dragons helped. The Clockwork Corridors were closed for now, and the only news came from Hilda as she brought more supplies through the hidden canal.

On the second day, Berin called everyone together again. She looked serious.

"Prince Harald is doing what he promised," she said. "He's organized a group to search the city, building by building, looking for the Guild Hall."

Mira and the others gulped.

"Will he find us?" asked Tom.

"No," said Berin. "We'll keep the secret passageways closed from now on, so there will be no way to get in. The underground canal comes out at a point far from the city center, where no one will find it. We'll just wait until they get tired of searching."

"How will we know?" asked Cara. "If we can't get in or out?"

Berin nodded. "Vice Chancellor?"

Vice Chancellor Creedy stepped forward.

Creedy was a stern, grumpy man and was usually scowling or making sharp comments about the children's dragon-riding skills. He was dragging a metal stand. Behind him came Daisy, the combat instructor, bouncy and jolly in green leggings so bright they almost glowed. She carried a massive silver bowl of water. Creedy positioned the stand, and Daisy placed the bowl on top.

"You will all be quiet," he announced in a harsh voice. Berin's lips twitched as if hiding a smile. He ignored everyone and bowed his head. After a few seconds, his dragon appeared.

Creedy's dragon was called Nightwatcher. She was large and a shining charcoal black. Even her teeth and tongue were black. The only color was in her eyes, which were bright red.

The children took a half step back.

Nightwatcher stretched her neck and peered into the silver bowl, closed her red eyes, and breathed gently on the water. It rippled and glowed. And then, against the back wall of the Guild Hall cavern, an image appeared.

It shimmered like a reflection, and at first it was too blurry to make out. Creedy rested one hand on Nightwatcher's neck, and she shifted. The picture focused.

"It's the city," murmured Ellis.

He was right. It was like seeing the city from a great height. Sunlight shone down, and Mira realized that she could even see tiny figures moving around.

"Oh!" she said. "It's like a camera obscura!"

"What's that?" asked Tom.

"A way of projecting an image," said Connor.

"It's really clever," said Mira. "You need a very small opening, and light comes in and gets projected against a—"

"Quiet!" hissed Creedy. He glared a beady eye at Mira.

"Sorry," muttered Mira.

Creedy and Nightwatcher concentrated, and the image moved, like a bird flying over Rivven. It swooped down to a market square. There was Prince Harald, talking to a group of men and women. They looked angry. There was no sound, but he was clearly sending them throughout the city.

"There," said Berin. "We can see where they are, and we're perfectly safe."

She smiled again, reassuringly. The image faded, and Berin dismissed the children. But as they turned away, Mira noticed Berin glancing up at the light globes. One globe was flickering softly.

Later, Berin came to visit them in the engine room.

"Do you know what the problem is?" she asked.

Grimbal looked harassed. "Not *absolutely*, no, Yer Ladyship," he muttered. "Got some ideas that I'm working through. Takes time to investigate something like this, you know."

Berin nodded. "How can we help?"

Grimbal shook his head. "Oh, I'm on top of it, don't you worry. Soon have it sorted. Yes."

"Maybe it's the Dragon's Heart," said Mira. "Maybe it's to do with that mark."

Berin looked at her sharply. "What?"

Grimbal rolled his eyes. "It ain't that. I've been checking—the Heart's fine. No, it's something in the workings. I've just got to nail it down." He waved a hand airily. "Girl's new. She doesn't know anything about anything yet."

"Hmm." Berin frowned. "Well, if you're *sure* . . ."

"Absolutely." Grimbal beamed. "Got an idea what it might be. Will sort it by tomorrow."

He waited until Berin had left. Then he turned to Mira and Flameteller.

"Don't you go telling bad ideas to Her Ladyship!" he snapped. "I been working this place since we found it—you think I don't know what's what?"

Mira was shocked. "No! I just thought we should consider all the—"

"Are you telling me I don't know my job?"

"No, I—"

"Get back to work!"

Mira stared at Grimbal. He was furious, but there was something else, she thought.

Almost . . . *fear*. He stormed out of the room.
Mira sighed and picked up her broom. The
Dragon's Heart continued its steady ticking.

"What was that about?" she asked
Flameteller.

"I don't know," said the dragon. "But there
is something wrong. I can feel it."

"I know! The way Grimbal's acting, it's
like—"

"No," interrupted the dragon. He sniffed
the air, as if picking up a scent. "I mean, in
here. Something . . . Can you hear it?"

"Hear what?" asked Mira. "It's pretty loud."

Flameteller shook his head. "All of this is
like a song to me," he said, waving a claw
up toward the mechanisms above their

heads. "Like music. But there's a wrong note somewhere. It's in the wrong place, or the wrong rhythm. . . ." He frowned. "I think it's coming from the Heart."

There was a clatter of metal as Grimbal returned with an armful of parts.

"Here," he said, dropping them on the floor. "Sort this all out, and no lip!"

"Yes, *sir*," muttered Mira.

When he left again, Mira whispered, "We should take a look."

"We can't," replied Flameteller. "Grimbal's here all day."

"Then we should take a look at *night*."

Flameteller hesitated, then nodded. They got to work.

That evening, Mira and Flameteller sat on the hut roof, waiting for everyone to go to sleep. More of the globes were flickering, Mira noticed. And every so often, a faint tremble ran through the cavern.

At midnight, they snuck down to the dock. Mira listened to the machinery, the lapping water of the canal, and the rush of the River Seek on the other side of the river wall, mighty and constant. There was nothing else.

They crept into the engine room and gazed at the great wheel.

"The bad note is coming from inside," said

Flameteller. "There's something wrong with the Heart, but I can't tell what it is."

"Could we take a quick peek?" asked Mira. She found the wrench Grimbal had used before and turned the dial that opened the cover. It was hard work, and Flameteller had to lean on the wrench with her. The metal screeched.

"It didn't do this before," whispered Mira. "I think the cover's swollen."

Finally it opened, and the glowing Dragon's Heart appeared.

Flameteller gazed at the dark stain. "It's definitely wrong. Can't you hear it?"

Mira listened. She tried to block out the

sounds of machinery. Yes . . . there was a faint whine. Actually, it was quite clear now. In fact, it seemed to be getting louder.

It was definitely getting louder.

"I think . . . ," she said slowly, "we should close the cover again."

The light from the Dragon's Heart had changed. It was brighter, she thought, but it was flickering. And the tick of its wheel seemed to be speeding up.

"I can almost hear what it's saying," muttered Flameteller. "Nearly. . . ."

Mira felt a sudden pang of alarm. "Close it," she said. "Close it now, Flame. Something's wrong. Close it!"

Flameteller blinked in surprise and then nodded. "Yes."

Mira lifted the wrench again. "Ready?"

Suddenly there was a crash behind them.

"What are you doing?" cried Grimbal. He was barefoot, wearing an old dressing gown and a nightcap.

"Sorry!" Mira blurted out. "We're just looking—"

"Get away from her!" he roared, and rushed toward them.

"We're trying to close it!"

"Away! Leave her alone!" He lunged at Mira, and she shrank back. The wrench was still in her hand.

"Stop!"

They collided, and the wrench swung back.

It hit the Dragon's Heart. . . .

And the Heart screamed.

8
DISASTER

"Argh!" shouted Mira, clapping her hands over her ears. The Dragon's Heart's scream was a metallic wail that was horrible to hear.

Grimbal stared in horror at the diamond face. "What have you done?" he gasped.

"Nothing!" protested Mira. "We were just looking!"

Beams of light pulsed from the Heart.

Flameteller said urgently, "We have to get out of here."

"No!" cried Grimbal. "We've got to close the cover!" He grabbed the wrench and tried to turn the dial, but it wouldn't move. The wailing was louder. "Come on!" he hissed. "Close!"

The noise was reaching a shriek, the light pulsing faster than ever. Mira staggered away, dizzy.

"Get away from there!" shouted Flameteller. Grimbal ignored him. Flameteller leaped forward and knocked him to the ground, and Grimbal turned in fury.

"You fool!" he shouted. "I got to—"

A beam of hot white-blue energy burst from

the Heart. It crackled with lightning and roared through the air where Grimbal had been standing, crashing right through the far wall. The workbench exploded, and bricks and dust flew.

Mira stared through the hole and across the canal, where the lightning had smashed into the ancient river wall. The stone slabs splintered under the pressure, mortar and dust flying everywhere, and the Dragon's Heart shrieked once more. Then the light stuttered and went out, and the Heart dimmed.

"Oh . . . ," moaned Grimbal.

Mira breathed out slowly in the new silence.

There was a sound like a *pop*, and a thin jet of water hissed out from between two battered slabs in the river wall. Mira watched it in horrified fascination. Hissssssssss . . .

"Oh, no," she murmured.

Then the river burst through.

A thousand gallons of frothing white water crashed through the wall, carving a large hole into the engine room. The mighty River Seek was coming in like the most powerful waterfall

Mira and Flameteller had ever seen. It poured
down into the canal. Water spread over the
dock. It was already at her feet!

"We're flooding!" she yelled. "We have to go!"

Grimbal scrambled to his feet. "Oh, no!" he wailed. "Oh, no!"

He ran toward a wooden box built into the wall and ripped off the cover. Inside was a long metal lever with a red handle. Grimbal heaved at it. "Help me!" he roared.

Mira and Flameteller pushed at the lever with him, and at last it moved. Next to the wall, weights dropped from the ceiling, and then from the near side of the canal, a tall metal barricade slid up. Mira saw that it was a flood barrier. The canal filled almost to the top of the barricade, a ferocious torrent of water, far too dangerous to enter.

Behind them, the Dragon's Heart ticked again, faster than ever, and the wheel around it spun. A new sound rang out above them. It was deep and huge, like a mechanical giant turning over in its sleep. When Grimbal heard it, he gasped.

"The Clockwork Corridors," he said. "They're out of control. They've opened up!" The wheel spun madly, screaming, faster and faster—

And stopped.

Everything stopped. All the machinery: the pulleys and ropes, crankshafts, conveyor belts, and fans. It was all quiet.

Above them, the dock globe lights faded out, and the world went dark.

"Oh, girl," whispered Grimbal's voice in the darkness. "What have you *done*?"

Grimbal found a lamp so they could wade over the flooded dock and up to the surface. As they made their way to and through the storerooms, Mira heard worried shouts. She saw little points of light that turned out to be people carrying lamps, rushing toward them. Berin reached them first. Lamplight swung shadows across her face.

"What happened?" she demanded.

Grimbal gaped at her. "They broke the Dragon's Heart!" he spat. "They *broke* it!"

Mira gasped. "I didn't mean to!" she squeaked. "It was *you*. You made me—"

"What about the Corridors?" asked Berin sharply. "Are they still working?"

Grimbal looked almost in tears. "*Nothing's* working," he gasped. "The Corridors are *open*!"

The others had caught up now, adults and children. Beside Berin, Creedy cursed. "If the passage is open, Prince Harald's knights can find us," he muttered. "We must evacuate."

"We *can't*," wailed Grimbal. "She broke the river wall too. The canal's impassable!"

Berin's face stayed calm. "Drun," she called into the darkness. "Make sure we have lamps and lamp oil for everyone. Vice Chancellor,

101

call up the scrying glass. I want to know where Prince Harald's mob is at all times. Daisy, prepare our defenses." Behind her, the adults scurried away at their tasks. Berin turned back. "Hilda, you and I will go with Mr. Grimbal to survey the damage."

"Yes, ma'am," said Hilda. Grimbal nodded, and they set off.

"Wait!" called Mira. "What can we do?"

"Get some rest," said Berin. She turned to the children and raised her lamp. "All of you, go back to bed. Nothing will happen until the morning."

"But we can help!" said Mira. "We can—"

"Enough!" snapped Berin. She shook her

head and sighed. "We need you to rest now. We'll discuss your actions later."

The adults left. Mira realized the other children were looking at her.

"Mira, what did you do?" asked Connor.

For a moment, Mira stared at him with her mouth open. Then she burst into tears.

9

RECOVERY

"And then suddenly there was this beam of—of *energy* or something," sobbed Mira. "And the river wall burst, and Grimbal was shouting. . . ."

She sat on her bed with the others around her. Erin held her hand. Connor shook his head.

"This is really bad," he said. "We can't close the passageways. We can't use the canal to escape. Without the fans, we might not even have enough fresh air. What were you thinking?"

"Enough," said Kai gently. He put a hand on Connor's shoulder. "Mira already feels bad; you don't need to rub it in."

Connor pursed his lips but didn't answer.

It was late, and eventually the boys returned to their dorm.

"Things will seem better in the morning," said Kai as he left. He gave Mira a small smile.

Erin and Cara crept into their bunks. Mira sat by the light of a lamp, staring at the wall.

It wasn't our fault, said Flameteller's voice. *We were trying to help.*

She nodded without answering and gazed

at Eliza the spider. Eliza was scurrying along Mira's headboard, and when she reached the end, she fell off and dangled by a silk thread.

"Oops," murmured Mira. "Let me give you a hand." She caught the thread and lifted it back up, but Eliza raced up in alarm and Mira jerked her hand back—straight into the web! It shriveled and tangled, and Eliza scurried away in fear.

"Oh, *no*," Mira whispered, staring at the knotted mess. "Eliza, I'm so sorry! Oh, I've ruined it! I've ruined *everything*!"

Mira, it's not your fault, tried Flameteller again. But Mira shook her head and broke their connection. Flameteller's voice disappeared.

She put out the lamp and lay in her bed, staring up into darkness.

Things will seem better in the morning, Kai had told her, but when Mira awoke, it was still dark.

At first she thought it was still night, but then she remembered—the globes weren't working, and without them the cavern would stay dark.

Erin and Cara weren't in the dorm. Mira lay in bed, wanting to stay there forever. But at last she sighed, lit her lamp, and got dressed. When she left, she saw flickering lanterns here and there, and a light coming from their dining hut. Mira wasn't hungry and couldn't face the others. She crept away.

Against the wall of the cavern, the shimmering picture of the city glowed. Creedy and Nightwatcher stood by their scrying glass, concentrating on the image. Outside, it was daylight. Most of the citizens were going about their work, but a crowd had gathered and was moving through the town. Prince Harald was leading them. Mira could see his flowing blond hair. The people stopped at each building to search. It wouldn't be long before they reached the entrance to the Guild Hall.

And with the Clockwork Corridors stuck wide open, they'd find it immediately.

Mira heard hammering ahead of her and saw more lamps. Daisy and Drun were building a barricade across the main doorway.

What would happen? Surely they could just talk to Prince Harald and find a way to prove they were friendly? Surely Berin could convince everyone they could trust the dragons! But she remembered Flameteller's words.

The humans are scared of us, he'd said. *Scared humans do strange things.*

She opened the path in her mind to let Flameteller through. He appeared, dipping his head onto her shoulder.

"Oh, Mira," he said. "I was so worried about you!"

Mira gulped. "I'm sorry for cutting you off. You're not angry, are you?"

The dragon laughed softly, and his warm breath surrounded her. "Of course not. You're my human."

Mira leaned against him and felt a little better. After a moment, she realized someone was coming toward her. It was Hilda, carrying a basket.

"Good morning, Mira, Flameteller," said Hilda cheerfully. "How are you today?"

Mira couldn't think how to answer that *at all*.

Hilda smiled. "Here." She reached into her basket and brought out a small pastry with a thick golden crust. "I'm bringing food around for the workers. Take one yourself."

Mira's stomach rumbled, but she hesitated. "Not me," she whispered. "I'm not a worker."

"Course you are," said Hilda. "You were working all day yesterday, and there's lots to do today."

"I don't . . . I don't think I deserve it," she murmured.

"Deary me." Hilda shook her head. "Let me tell you two things, my darling. First, *everyone* deserves a nice pastry now and then, and I won't have you turning one down."

Mira smiled shyly. Hilda's pastries were famous, and this one was still warm, with steam rising from it in the cold cavern air.

"And second," said Hilda, setting down her basket, "this is my own special recipe. It took me seventeen goes to get it right. You got to get the right filling, and the right consistency, and the right kind of dough, and you got to cook it just right, and season it, and, oh, any amount of other things. Sixteen times I got it wrong. One time I set the oven on fire! Adults mess up just as often as children, let me tell you. And we're not so good at learning. So you take this, and you eat it and build your strength up. And if you broke something, figure out how to fix it or how to help.

"But don't—and this is important, child, so listen—don't, *ever*, turn down one of Hilda Brugarden's famous pastries again." She grinned.

Despite herself, Mira laughed. "Sorry," she said, and took it. It smelled delicious.

"There," said Hilda. "Much better. Now, find yourself a space, eat up, and when you're ready, come and join us. It'll be fine."

"Thank you," said Mira. Hilda nodded, picked up her basket, and walked away.

Mira still didn't feel she could face the others in the dining hut, so she headed back to her dorm and ate the pastry there. It was fantastic, hot and sweet. Suddenly she felt better. Flameteller sat on the floor next to her bed. Dragons didn't need to eat in this world, but he liked the smell.

"What am I going to do?" she asked, sighing.

The dragon shrugged. "What *can* we do?" he asked. "What happened with the Dragon's Heart?"

"I wish I knew," said Mira.

"I could hear it," said Flameteller. "It was like it was trying to tell me something. All of it, the wheel, the mechanism. . . ." He slapped a paw on the floor in frustration, raising a cloud of dust, and then sneezed. For a moment, he looked so silly that Mira laughed.

"Hey," he said, looking past her. "Look at Eliza."

Mira turned and saw the little spider's web

by her bed. Eliza had been busy overnight. The torn patch of web was still there, but she'd spun new silk around it, making wider circles and repairing most of the damage. The web wasn't perfect, but it was good again.

"Oh, thank goodness," said Mira. "Eliza,

I thought I'd ruined your web as well as everything else!"

"All she needed was a bit of time to recover," said Flameteller.

Mira nodded. Then she stopped. "Oh," she murmured. "That's it. That's *it*."

"What?" asked Flameteller.

Mira's heart sang. "That's it, Flameteller! I know what's wrong! Come on!" She stuffed the last of the pastry into her mouth, grabbed her lamp, and raced for the door. "Hurry!"

Flameteller scrambled to get up. "What is it? Where are we going?"

"We'll need help!" shouted Mira. "Come on! Oh, we can fix it, we can *fix* it!"

10
OLD NEW WAYS

Mira raced toward the dining hut and reached it just as the others were leaving. They were quiet, and when they saw her, they looked wary.

"We let you sleep in," said Erin. "We thought you needed your rest."

Connor rolled his eyes. "Yes, after what you achieved yesterday."

Mira ignored him. "Everyone, I need your help," she said.

They stared at her.

"That's it?" asked Connor. "Not even *I'm sorry*?"

Mira sighed. "Connor, I'm sorry. I was trying to help, and there was an accident. It wasn't my fault, but it happened because I was there, so I'm sorry. But I know *why* it happened! And I know what we have to do!"

They looked at each other. "Okay," said Tom at last. "Why did it happen?"

"Flameteller made me realize," said Mira. "And the dust. There *is* something wrong with the Dragon's Heart. Flameteller says it *sounds* wrong. And it's too hot and swollen.

It's been struggling, and sometimes it's out of control. . . ." Mira took a deep breath. "I think it's *sick*."

"What?" Connor frowned. "Mira, it's a thing, not an animal. I mean, I know it's magic, but it can't get *sick*."

"How do you know?" asked Mira.

Connor glanced at Kai. "What do you think?"

Kai was interested in medicine. He looked thoughtful. "It does sound like an infection. But the explosion?"

"I think that was a *sneeze*," said Mira.

"Huh," said Kai. "Maybe. It might have been a convulsion—that happens sometimes if you get a fever." He nodded. "It's possible."

Connor raised his hands. "Even if that's true, how do we cure a magic object?"

"I have no idea," said Mira. "But maybe we don't need to. It's over a thousand years old, so it must be pretty good at looking after itself. Maybe we just need to give it time to recover."

"We don't have time," said Cara. "Prince

Harald's knights are getting close, and we can't move the passageways."

"We tried this morning," said Tom. "Even the dragons can't turn the machinery."

"But maybe we can find something else," said Mira. "Like an alternative power source, just enough so we can let the Heart recover. I've got an idea, but I'll need your help."

She told them what she had in mind. Connor scratched his chin. "Doubtful."

"It will work," said Mira. "*Trust me*. Come on—the adults are all busy. We're just sitting and waiting, but we could fix things!"

The others hesitated, and Mira's heart sank. But then Erin sighed.

"Mira," she said. "You're exhausting, and

you talk too much, and you break things *a lot*.
But you've always got interesting ideas. All
right, then—count me in!"

Tom grinned. "Me too." Even Connor
sighed and nodded.

"All right," said Mira. "Let's go and save the
Guild."

The young dragonseers and their dragons
crept through the storerooms and down to the
dock.

Grimbal wasn't there. Mira wondered if he
was trying to get the Clockwork Corridors
working. Tom lifted his lamp and whistled

at the mess. The dock was almost destroyed, and the workshop floor was underwater. Barrels and ropes floated or lay scattered like wreckage on a beach. The canal roared with white water, but everything else was quiet— no moving machinery, no ticking from the Dragon's Heart.

"This way," whispered Mira.

The Heart's cover was still open. Its face throbbed with an unsteady, slightly yellow light. The wheel around it moved and stopped, moved and stopped, like the hand of a clock that had nearly wound down. It was trying to turn, but it was too weak. Mira put out her hand and patted the covering. She didn't dare touch the Heart itself.

Connor peered through the hole in the engine room.

"That was some sneeze," he said.

"Prince Harald's moving again," called Ellis. He had positioned himself on a dry spot on the dock, listening for Cara. Cara was listening for her dragon, Silverthief—and Silverthief, who could stay hidden and even invisible, was up in the Guild Hall, watching the scrying image on the wall. Together they formed a human-dragon chain, sharing reports.

"He's close!" called Ellis. "He's reached our part of town."

"So what do we do?" asked Erin.

Mira looked at Flameteller. "What do you think?" she asked.

"I can hear the mechanism," the dragon muttered. "It *wants* to move. If we can connect everything up, it might work—"

"Grimbal's coming!" called Ellis suddenly from behind them.

"Hide!" shouted Mira.

But it was too late—he was already stomping through the workshop. "What're you lot doing here?" he demanded. "Get back to where you belong!" Erin and Ellis looked at each other but didn't move as Grimbal passed them.

He entered the engine room and glared at Mira and Flameteller. *"You two!"* he gasped. "Ain't you done enough damage?"

Mira raised her hands. "Mr. Grimbal, I'm trying to help—"

"Like last time? Look what you did!"

Mira nodded. "I know, but I've got an idea—"

"You don't know what you're doing!" he shouted. "You ain't got a clue!"

"Well, neither do *you*!" she snapped.

Grimbal blinked. "How dare you—" he started, but Mira kept going.

"You *knew* the Dragon's Heart was sick, didn't you?" she demanded. "You knew, and you didn't know how to fix it!"

"Well, I—"

"All that stuff you said to Berin about ideas you had—that was all made up! Admit it— you don't know what to do!"

Grimbal glared at her. He stood up to his

126

full height. "Young lady," he started. "I . . . I . . ."

And then he stopped. His shoulders slumped, and he seemed to deflate. The angry crease on his forehead lifted into one of helplessness. He collapsed into a chair and sagged.

"It's been happening for months," he moaned. "Just a bit at first. I think . . . I think she's *dying*."

Mira gaped at him. "Why didn't you *tell* someone?"

"You don't know what it's like!" he protested. "They're all depending on me, like I know how to fix everything!" His head sank. "But I don't. I don't know what to do."

The children stared at each other. Hesitantly, Mira patted his shoulder. "It's okay," she said. "I have a plan. We just need a source of power."

"But we don't have one!" wailed Grimbal.

"Well, actually we do. . . ." Mira turned and pointed out through the hole in the wall to the raging river behind them. She grinned.

"We can build a *waterwheel*."

For a moment, Grimbal's face brightened, but then he shook his head.

"Don't be daft, child. There's no waterwheel in the world as strong as the Heart!"

"But we don't need that much power," said Mira. "All we need is enough to move the Corridors for now. Just enough to give the Dragon's Heart time to recover. I think it *can* recover."

She looked at Grimbal. "I don't know if I'm right. And I don't know how to build a waterwheel. I'll need your help. But we can *try*, can't we?"

Grimbal scowled and chewed his lip, gazing at the Dragon's Heart and its weak light. Then he nodded and stood. "All right," he said. "We can try."

"Prince Harald's only two streets away!" shouted Ellis.

Mira lifted her chin. "Let's get started."

11
FLAMETELLER

Grimbal and Mira gave the orders, and the children and their dragons got to work— Tom and mighty Ironskin, Kai and solid Boneshadow, Connor and clever Lightspirit. Erin couldn't summon Rockhammer by herself, so she settled for shouting orders at everyone else's dragons and insisting on carrying the heaviest of everything.

"We'll need an axle," said Mira. "And somewhere to hold it on either side."

"There are mooring pins on the river wall," said Grimbal, pointing. "There and there. But they won't hold for long."

"We only need a little time," said Mira.

"We could use the main shaft from the Heart," muttered Grimbal. He scribbled down calculations with a pencil. "It's long enough, I reckon. . . ."

"We'll need blades for the wheel. And something to build a wheel out of."

"What type should we go for?" he asked. "Overshot, backshot?"

Mira thought. "Backshot, if we can," she said thoughtfully. "More efficient, with less—"

"Less turbulence," he finished, and nodded. "Good thinking, lass." Mira beamed. Grimbal turned to the others. "Right, you lot!" he shouted. "We need flat pieces of wood, and poles to make wheel spokes out of! Anything you can find!"

They raced over the workshop and dock, looking for anything they could use.

"What about doors?" asked Connor. "We could break the doors into parts."

"Good thinking!" shouted Mira.

"I've found the remains of the barge!" called Erin. "It's all smashed up, but there are lots of flat pieces!"

"Bring them here!" called Mira. She chewed her lip. "We don't have much time."

They hammered and sawed, tied and fastened. Cara and Ellis sent them reports from upstairs. The adults were forming lines of defense. Prince Harald's mob was only a street away now. They had to hurry. It was a terribly rushed job. Would it work?

"Ready!" called Mira. "Ironskin, give us a hand!"

The huge dragon leaned down to help the others heave the wheel up onto its edge.

"It looks pretty rough," said Connor doubtfully.

Mira nodded. "It'll have to do. We'll roll it across now. Ready?"

"Wait!" said Flameteller suddenly. "One of the spokes is loose—I can hear it!"

They found the piece and tightened it. The dragon nodded. "It wants to work, but it's fragile."

"Come on!" called Grimbal.

Together they rolled the wheel to the edge of the canal. The dragons lifted it into the air, beating their wings hard, and carried it over the water.

"Okay, very slowly: lower!" ordered Mira. She was worried. Once the wheel was moving, it would be okay, but when it first touched the raging current . . . They lowered it, but then Flameteller roared, "Back up!"

They lifted it again. Flameteller said, "The river's too fast! The wheel can't hold; it's too weak. It's *scared*."

Mira gazed at him. "You can really *hear* that?"

Flameteller looked surprised. "Yes," he said. "Can't you?"

"No," said Mira. "No one can. Flame . . . I think this might be your *power*. You can hear machinery. . . ." She stopped. "Can you *talk* to it?"

The dragon tipped his head to one side. "I'm not sure. . . . Perhaps?"

"Try!" said Mira. "Talk to it! Persuade it to hold together or something—just until it starts spinning!"

Flameteller gazed at her. His wings beat in the air—those curious wings, with their brown-bronze markings that made him look a bit like a machine himself.

"I think I can do that," he said softly. He closed his eyes and stretched, and seemed to grow larger. Then he made a noise like the rumble of gears, or the clatter of pulleys, or the squeal of belts. It was like a song, in a strange language like nothing Mira had ever heard, and yet one that seemed as familiar as a dream. It was a song of strength, and holding tight, and working together. . . .

"Now," he murmured. The dragons lowered

the axle into the water, and the wheel spun furiously. The wooden slats and spokes creaked and rattled, but held. And all the time Flameteller sang to the wheel, encouraging it, telling it how well it was doing, keeping it together.

"It's in place!" roared Grimbal. "Get the belt!"

The children lined up the belt that would connect the wheel shaft to the Clockwork Corridors.

"Ready?" called Mira. "Contact!"

There was a shriek of gears and a squeal as the belt attached to the spinning shaft. Would it hold? Flameteller sang to it again as it skidded and squealed. Finally it gripped and

139

started turning with the shaft. Above them, the great mechanism started shifting, and the pulleys moved and ropes whipped past and wheels spun.

"They're on the street!" called Ellis. "Prince Harald is on the street! They're only two houses away!"

"Will it work?" asked Mira.

Grimbal stared at the workings. "It's going to be close . . . ," he whispered.

They waited for a few agonizing moments.

"They're at the cottage!" shouted Ellis.

That was when, far away, they heard a *clunk*. Then there was a loud mechanical noise and a whir. Grimbal smiled and closed his eyes.

"That was it," he murmured. "That was it. The passage is closed."

Mira let her head sink in relief. She felt as if she could sleep for a week.

 141

"They've moved on to the next house," called Ellis. "They've moved on!"

All around Mira the machinery hummed and danced and clattered and roared and found its rhythm. Flameteller sang along.

"You did it," she whispered.

"*We* did it," he murmured, and continued with his song. Behind them, the Dragon's Heart grew dim, and its cover closed, and it went to sleep.

12
NEW OLD
WAYS

It was a special occasion, so Grimbal was wearing his best brown coat. Mira grinned when she saw him enter the engine room.

"Looking sharp, Mr. G," she said, and he nodded.

"Thank you. Are we ready?" he asked.

"They're coming down now," Mira said.

Grimbal nodded again. He seemed a little distracted.

It was a few weeks later, and the workshop and dock were almost restored. The canal was still raging, and the hole in the river wall still gaped, but the flood barricade had held.

"Have you been tidying?" Mira asked.

"Well, you know, just here and there," Grimbal mumbled. His cheeks turned pink in embarrassment.

Mira smiled. "Looks good. Here they come now."

A procession came down the stairs, lamps bobbing as they walked: Chancellor Berin first; then Vice Chancellor Creedy; then Hilda, Drun, and Daisy; and finally the children. They entered the engine room.

"Good afternoon, Mr. Grimbal," said Berin.

Grimbal bowed. "Yer Ladyship."

"Are we all ready?"

Grimbal and Mira glanced at Flameteller, and he nodded. Berin smiled.

"Very well," she said. "Begin."

Grimbal walked over to the wall where the Dragon's Heart sat in the center of the frozen wheel. He opened the main panel and lifted his wrench to the dial. Hesitating, he turned to Mira.

"Here, lass," he said, offering her the wrench. "You do it."

Mira gulped. Carefully, she turned the dial to open the cover. Slowly, it opened, just a line at first, then two parts, pulling apart . . . and there was the Dragon's Heart. It pulsed slowly, with only a faint light. But the light was clean and pure now, and there was no stain.

"She's feeling much better," said Grimbal happily. "She went to sleep once we disconnected. Just needed a bit of time to recover."

Berin smiled. "I'm very pleased to hear that." She stepped forward and touched the tip of her staff against the diamond face. The tip glowed blue, and the Dragon's Heart glowed back clear and strong, brighter and brighter. Around it, the wheel started moving in a steady tick, and the shaft behind it turned, and cogs whirred.

Above them, the globe lights lit up with their calm, soft glow.

Erin started cheering, and the adults clapped. Even Vice Chancellor Creedy gave a pale smile. Berin turned to Mira, Flameteller, and Grimbal, and bowed.

"Well done," she said.

Mira blushed.

"And the waterwheel?" asked Berin.

Mira nodded. "Now the Heart's better, we can disconnect the wheel. And then we can repair the wall and get the canal back to normal."

"And will the Heart be all right from now on?" Berin turned to look at Grimbal.

"Should be," said Grimbal. "Course, I don't know everything. Still a few tricks I could learn, I reckon." He winked at Mira. "But if the old girl needs a rest, we can put the waterwheel back for a bit, now and then."

"It's always good to have an alternative," said Berin.

Later, Berin sat in her office with Mira and Flameteller.

"Grimbal suggested you run the project to repair the river wall," she said.

Mira grinned. "I'd love to!" she said. "I was thinking we can put in a gate and an adaptable wheel. Then, when we need to, we can increase the water pressure and generate additional power, and then—"

Berin lifted a hand. "I'm sure you'll do a good job," she said, smiling. She nodded to Flameteller. "And congratulations on your new power!"

The dragon purred with happiness. "Thank you," he said, bowing his head.

"A dragon who can hear the songs of machinery," Berin said thoughtfully. "A dragon who can *sing* to machinery . . ." Her cheeks creased. "Drun is very excited about that. He says he doesn't know how to classify you. He thinks you might be something never seen before." She nodded. "Perhaps you're *both* something new."

She stood and walked to the window.

"This is the Dragonseer Guild," she said. "Here for over a thousand years. And although we are new to it, we are all trying to learn from the old ways."

She smiled at Mira. "But not *just* the old ways. We must learn some new ways of our own, even we ancient ones. What did Grimbal say? Still a few tricks we could learn? We try to teach you young dragonseers what we know. But perhaps . . . we need you to teach us what *you* know too?"

"Maybe we should run a class," Mira said with a grin.

Berin laughed. "Possibly! Thank you, Mira."

Mira hesitated. "Miss?"

"Hmm?"

"What's going to happen outside?"

Berin sighed. "The mob died down when Prince Harald found nothing. But King Godfic knows we're here somewhere. He believes we have stolen something from his very chambers. He is scared, and scared humans do strange things. And there are other mysteries—the other dragon Tom saw near the palace, the fact that the king even *had* a Dragon's Eye. . . . Something is going on, and we must all be on our guard."

Mira nodded.

Berin smiled. "But that's a problem for another day. Go! Take today off, and report to Grimbal tomorrow for your new project."

Mira bowed. "Yes, miss."

She walked back to the dormitory with Flameteller.

"That was nice," he said, stretching his neck for her to scratch.

Mira smiled. "Yes."

"So what shall we do now?" asked the dragon. "Take today off?"

"Sure," said Mira. "Or . . . maybe we could visit the engine room, just for a little bit. There might be something that needs fixing."

"Good idea," said Flameteller. They made their way to the workshop. Then Flameteller sang his song to the machines, and the machines sang back.